To my twins Zac and Bella, you are the grea
I love you soooo......Much!

First published in Great Britain in 2021

ISBN 978-1-8383415-0-3

Rufus finds more time

by Astrid Schmitt-Bylandt

Illustrated by Alex Crump

Have you ever been to **Haste Hill?**
Yes, it's really called **Haste** Hill. It is quite close to London, near a place called Ruislip. The area is so beautiful – it has truly magical woodland that you would never imagine existing anywhere so close to a big city like London.

You will have to visit it one day and see it with your own eyes otherwise you might just not believe me. So, it is here, that a little squirrel called Rufus lives.

Rufus loves the woods and he especially loves the big man-made lake with its own beach. It's close to his home - a beautiful big oak tree, not far from Haste Hill Station. But most of all he loves the wonderful little "choo choo trains" that run past his home nearly every day. They run from "Willow Lawn Station" and go all the way to "Woody Bay Station" and back, through the beautiful woodland. You'll think you're in a fairy-tale country when you take a ride on one of the wonderful little trains... and maybe you just are!

There are six different trains and Rufus knows them all so well, that even with his eyes closed, he can tell who is whizzing past his tree.
Sometimes it's the black and green 'Mad Bess', with her steam engine. She makes a very distinctive sound and she is definitely Rufus' favourite. Then there is the blue 'Graham Alexander', and the yellow and blue 'Robert' -, and then of course you have the dark red and yellow 'Lady of the Lakes', and let's not forget the little green and white 'Bayhurst.'
Lastly, there is also the dark red and yellow 'John Rennie' a diesel mechanical and Rufus' second favourite as it's really fast.

Year in year out, loads of people visit the beautiful little lake and beach area. They take in some sun, play on the beach and, of course, go for a long walk in the peaceful woods.

Rufus could see it was making people very happy to breathe the fresh air, to relax and leave all thoughts of work and worries behind for a few hours. Sometimes he could even see film crews setting up early mornings. He was of course very curious as to what they were filming, and if you ever watch a film made at the lake and beach, see if you can spot Rufus hiding in the back!

Being so close to London, many people enjoy their time here. However, with all those visitors the area started to become... dirtier. People sometimes leave their food, bottles and rubbish lying around and the little squirrel tries hard to keep the area clean.
In the evenings, when everyone has gone home and the humans have parked all the trains for the night, Rufus and his two best friends Chichi the Mouse and Randolph the Rabbit, ride on the trains up and down the tracks, scooping up all the rubbish people had dropped along the railway line.

Oh, and what fun they had riding on the trains! As “Mad Bess” is Rufus’ favourite she always gives the loudest ‘chooioooooo’ when Rufus and his friends come to visit her in the evenings, for one last run for the day.

Can you imagine though, not only do people throw rubbish wherever they sit or play, but they also throw their rubbish into the lake. Can you believe that?

Slowly over the years, this has started to affect the quality of the water. Rufus knows that plastic does not rot, so he has started to worry that over time the pollution that all the rubbish was causing, would damage not just the lake and beach, but also the beautiful countryside he and his friends were living in.

Being a squirrel Rufus was very fast and always very busy, which I guess is why he chose to live in Haste Hill. But it was a huge task for a little squirrel, a rabbit, and a tiny mouse. The three of them were often tired in the evenings from running around, working so hard to keep the area clean. Nevertheless, they truly loved it!

One sunny Sunday Rufus had a visitor from central London. It was his old friend, the wise grey squirrel Archibald, who lived under the eaves of the Houses of Parliament in central London.

Archibald was amazed by how much work Rufus and his two friends had put into keeping this whole area as clean as possible. He also loved hearing their stories on life around the lake as these were always interesting and sometimes very funny. He thanked Rufus, Chichi and Randolf for the amazing voluntary work they were doing.

"If everyone could do a bit of volunteering and helping out", he said, "then we would all spread a little more happiness". "Isn't that a really worthwhile and very easy thing to do?"

Yes", said Chichi with a big grin, "one kind act a day blows the darkness away"!!

They all laughed and turned to Archie as every time Archie came to visit, he too told them the most amazing and sometimes crazy stories of the buzzing capital. About the big house he lived in, and how lots of humans were always sitting opposite each other talking, debating, laughing and sometimes even shouting at each other.

"They talk about all sorts of topics", Archie said, "once, they even had a debated for hours about hedgehogs! "About me", said Helga the hedgehog slightly blushing, "I didn't know we were so important, that makes me a little proud", she said and beamed.

Archie had seen many people come and go and some of his stories were very funny too, so Rufus and his friends were also always looking forward to a visit from Archie and so they all took a stroll through the beautiful woods.

Archie admired all the trees and bushes along the way. Every now and then he asked Rufus, “What berries are these?” and, “What kind of tree is that?” “I really don’t come out here often enough”, said Archie “can you teach me a little bit more about nature?”
Rufus shrugged his shoulders. “I don’t know a lot about the trees and the bushes” he said. “Oh, that is so sad,” said Archibald, “You live in this magical area, I think you should try and make some time to learn about the trees, the plants, and the environment you live in. Don’t you think?” He winked at Rufus with a cheeky smile. “Yes,” said Rufus laughing, “You are absolutely right! I will try and make some time each week, but I am so busy at the moment I don’t know how to find the time?” “Never just say ‘I will try’”, said Archie. “Do it! don’t just try!” “If you really want something, then make a commitment, if only to yourself!”

Rufus had learned all about the things he needed for eating, like the hazelnut bush and the acorns from the Oak trees. He knew how to pick his meals and he knew which bushes not to touch, for they were poisonous, - like the Ivy!

But he hadn't really ever thought it necessary to continue learning more. He had everything he needed after all, right?

Do you think he could have made a little more time to learn a bit more?
*Do you think he **should** take more the time to learn more?*

"Archie, you're right," said Rufus, "I live in this beautiful area. I really need to make time to study and learn more! Afterall, I can then share this knowledge with everyone. But when? And how?"

"Ah..." said Archibald in a low voice, sounding even a little bit secretive. "Only when you focus on what you really want and what is important in your life, can you find more time for the things you want to do! You will see! Then you will shift your daily habits alongside."

"But how?" asked Rufus.
"Very easy" said Archie, "you just have to make a plan! A written one!
Write everything down! Every day! Then focus and take action! Every single day!
You will be amazed at how much time you will find..." replied Archie.

Rufus was puzzled. How can you "find" time? Time wasn't something that you could find under a tree leaf or near a hazelnut bush? But Archie was older and wiser and Rufus really loved and respected the old squirrel, so he vowed to give this some thought.

There were however things that Rufus did know! The lake was home to ducks, Canada geese, and Mute swans who had all become Rufus, Randolph, and Chichi's friends. They all helped take the litter from the water in their beaks and bring it to the beach, so the trio could then collect it and drop it in the bins.
They loved working in teams and named themselves the "Dry Land Team" or "DLT" and the "Wet Water Team" or "WWT". Sometimes they would even race each other to see which team would finish first. This way, work was just more fun!

DLT
WWT

Often, they would all sit and prepare a lovely picnic in a little corner of the beach after all the cleaning work was done for the day. They would tell each other stories of the people they had seen and the funny things that had happened that day or that week.

Sometimes a few local animals, would join in. In the evenings even some of the local bats started flying over, to listen to everyone's stories.

“I saw this big man on a lilo today, his feet were dangling over the side. I just couldn’t pass up the opportunity to nibble on his toes… just a little bit, and with a big WOSH he fell into the water!” “Did you see that?” asked Samuel the swan.

“Haha - yes I did,” chuckled Chuck the old Canada goose. “I saw that!”
“The guy made a right big splash!”

“I saw a little girl with a toy crocodile today”, quacked Dina the Duck. “The crocodile was getting away from her, so I just gave it a little nudge to push it back. She thought the crocodile had come alive, and she was so excited that it made me chuckle.”

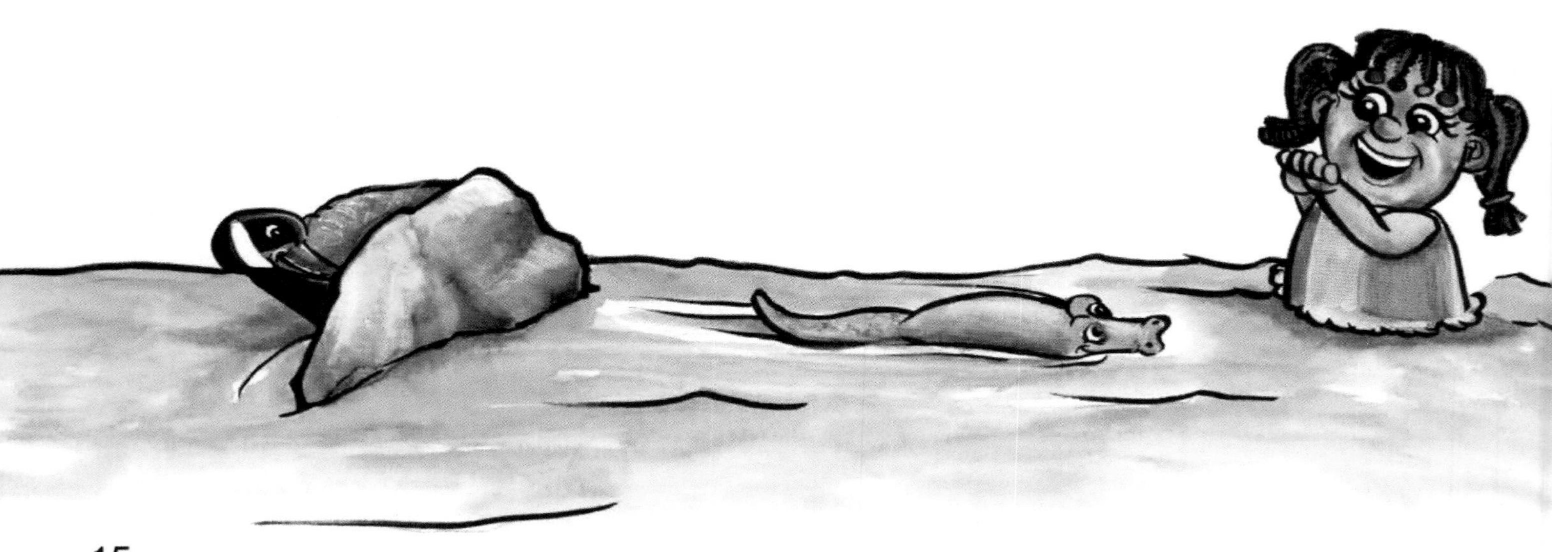

When Archibald had left that evening, Rufus was lying awake for a long time under his hazelnut leaf, up in his little house in the old Oak tree. He was looking at the starlit sky and for the first time in his life, he really took the time to study the sky in detail.

"Wow," he thought, "I never realised just how many stars there are in the sky and how they change from spring to summer to autumn and to winter. I wonder why that is?" He vowed to find out over the next few days and with those thoughts in mind, Rufus fell asleep with a happy smile on his face.

Life was good at the lake and the woodlands, but then one day, people stopped coming.
The beach was empty, and the very few people who did come through the woods were wearing some funny masks on their faces. Rufus had never seen these things before.

The squirrel found a packet with one of those masks on the ground and thought it would make a great hammock. So, as fast as he could, he set up a little corner in his garden for the new hammock. For the first time, Rufus enjoyed the fact that he didn't have to live in haste cleaning up, as there was nothing to clean up.

Rufus realised over the next weeks, that the air was getting better and the water from the lake was becoming clearer too.
“I do miss the people and buzz!”, Rufus thought, “but life is good when you are actually able to slow down a little bit”.
Rufus had been used to gulping down half a hazelnut in the morning with a hazelnut coffee which was still a bit too hot,- he always burnt his mouth a little, silly Rufus right?

Now he had a whole hazelnut in peace and quiet for breakfast and actually enjoyed his coffee at the right temperature. Afterwards he went for a run around the lake.

Never had Rufus felt so fit and relaxed and it really made him happy.
One morning, as he was enjoying his run around the lake, he suddenly thought of old Archie and his words, “Only when you focus on what you really want and what is important to you, can you find more time.”

“TIME,” thought Rufus. “I now have a lot of time!”

And so, he began to read and study. First, he started learning about the trees and the bushes in his area.
He was lying in his newly found hammock devouring the books he had found about the local trees.
“Oaks and Hornbeams…he read aloud.. haha! Hornbeams… that’s a funny name - do these trees really have horns?” “No, but of course they don’t, it still sounds funny!”

“Ha, and so there are also, English Oak, Sessile Oak, Beech, Silver Birch, Wild Service Tree, Aspen, Rowan, Field Maple, Crack Willow, Wild Cherry, Hazel, and Holly.

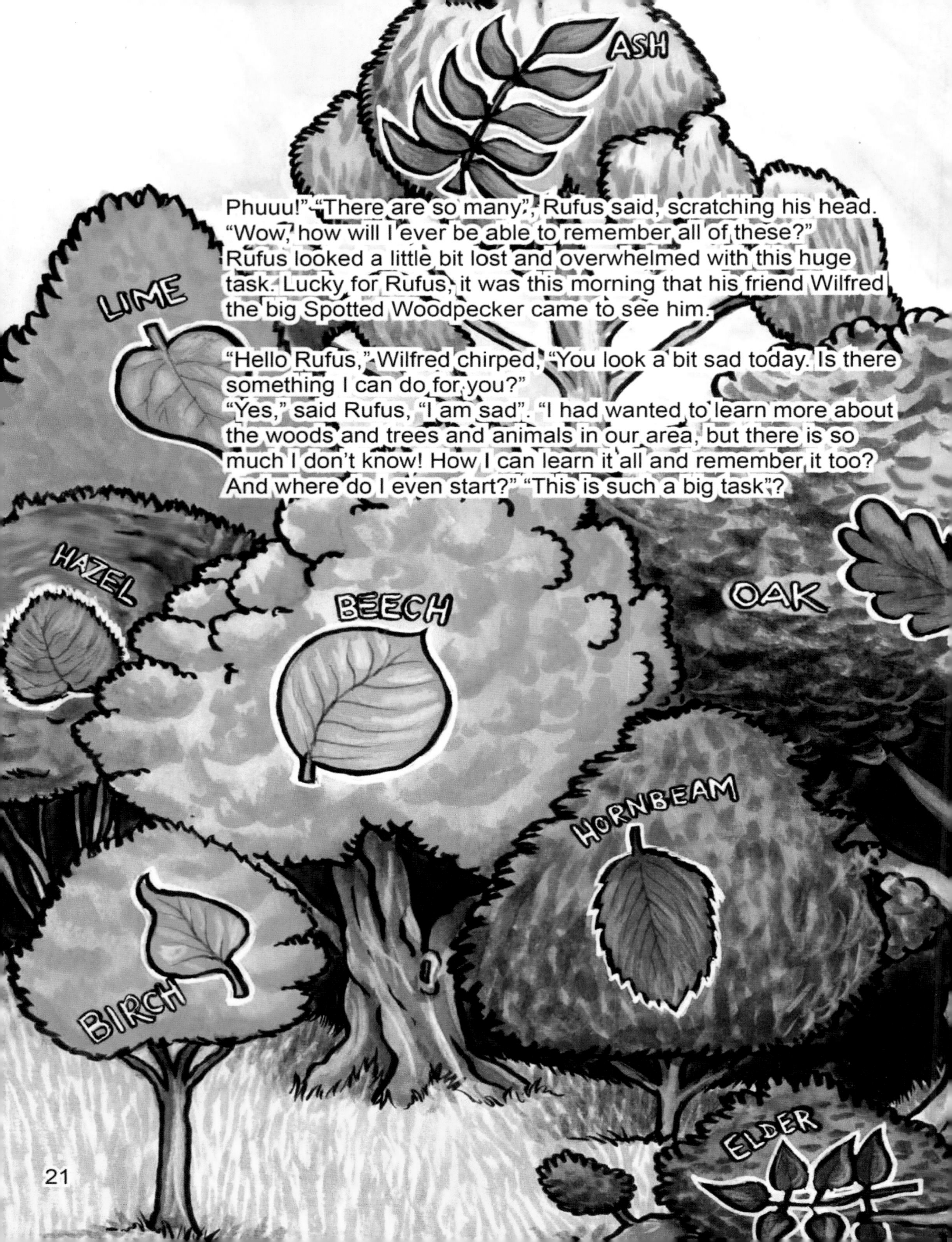

Phuuu!" "There are so many", Rufus said, scratching his head. "Wow, how will I ever be able to remember all of these?" Rufus looked a little bit lost and overwhelmed with this huge task. Lucky for Rufus, it was this morning that his friend Wilfred the big Spotted Woodpecker came to see him.

"Hello Rufus," Wilfred chirped, "You look a bit sad today. Is there something I can do for you?"
"Yes," said Rufus, "I am sad". "I had wanted to learn more about the woods and trees and animals in our area, but there is so much I don't know! How I can learn it all and remember it too? And where do I even start?" "This is such a big task"?

“That’s an easy one,” said Wilfred and gave a big grin. “It so happens I am an expert in all the trees and shrubs. If you want, I can help you?”

Rufus’ face brightened. “Yes!” he said, “Together this task will be so much easier! Thank you, I will gladly take you up on your offer. When can we start?”
“Right away,” said Wilfred and he spread his wings. “See that tree across the other side of the path? That’s an Oak tree.. and he pointed out to the leaf of the tree with its very distinct shape.

Every morning from then on, Rufus brought his books for their study session and Wilfred kept his promise. Together they jumped and flew through the woods comparing the leaves of the trees, with the ones in the books. Wilfred pointed out the various plants and after a few days he started testing Rufus.

“Eeek..are you testing me?”, said Rufus with a pretend expression of shock in his face. “Haha, yes I am, said Wilfred, but you have done incredibly well! “Well, said Rufus, having someone like you helping me, made me learn twice as fast. Thank you so, so much!

“And you know what is so crazy? If only I had known you earlier! In fact, I should have known you when I went to Forest School. I would have done so much better in Miss Arduous’ Greenery Class!” He smiled as he remembered how she despaired when Randolph, Chichi, and Rufus had accidentally set the hazelnut bush at the back of the school lab on fire. It had caused a big puff of smoke and a lot of dark black soot had covered all their faces, including that of Miss Arduous’, who, as you can imagine, didn’t seem to be all too pleased!

As Rufus was getting into this whole new world of learning and studying, Wilfred had introduced him to Willy the Weasel. Willy was the best help for all the plants and bushes on the ground.

"We have Fern, Common Knapweed, Harebell, Rosebay, Willowherb, Heather, Bluebell, Woodanemone, Yellow Archangel, Snowdrops, and Honeysuckle," said Willy. "Shall we go and explore and I will point them all out to you?"
"Yes please", said Rufus. He was so happy, every day was more fun and even his friend Chichi had started to join them, which made it even more fun.

ROSEBAY
WILLOWHERB
HAREBELL
KNAPWEED
SNOWDROP
BLUEBELL
DAISY
HEATHER

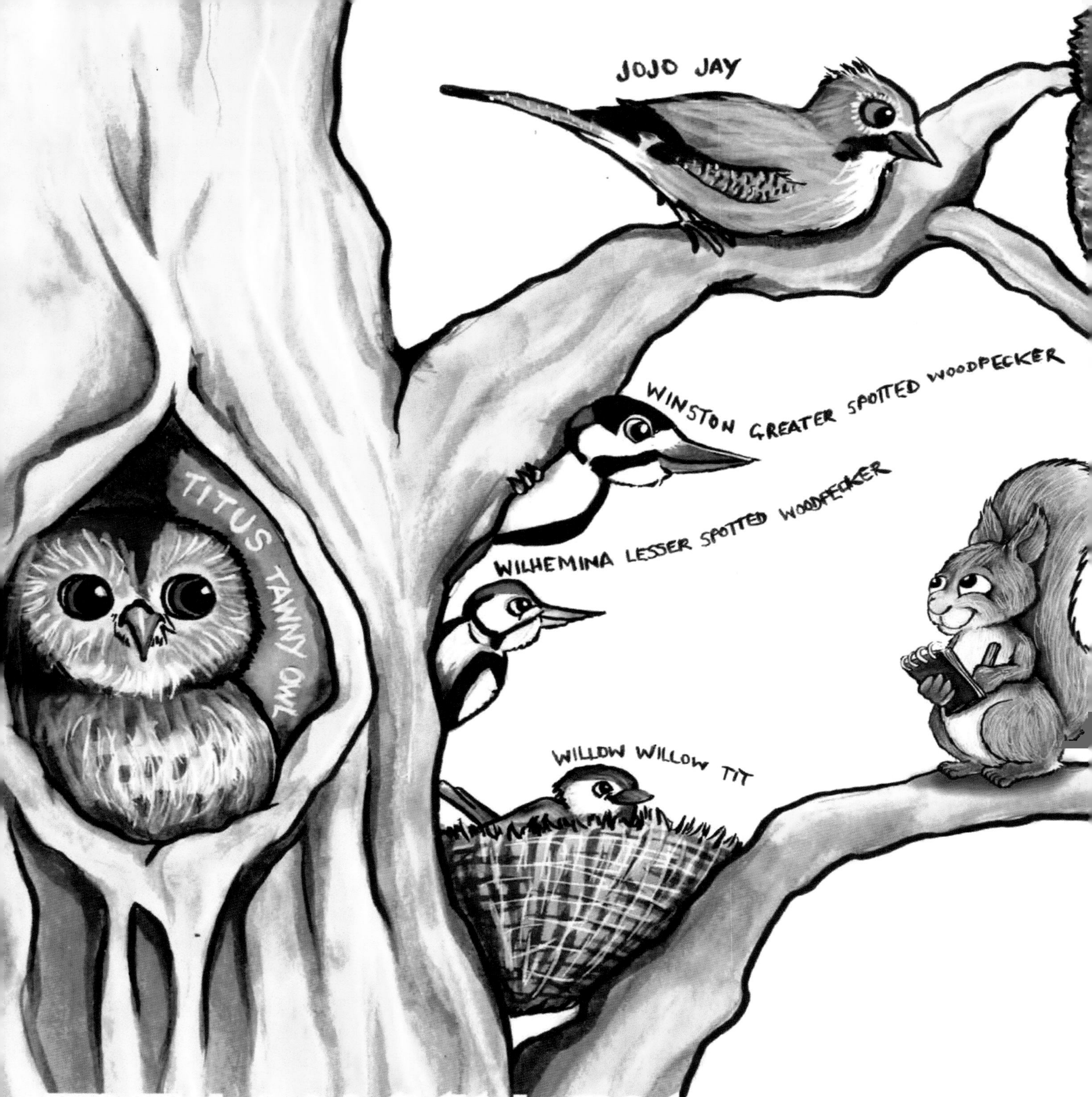

Wilfried Woodpecker had not just introduced Rufus to Willy the Weasel but also to some of his bird friends.
There was, Runa the Robin, Winston the Green Woodpecker, Jojo the Jay, Nora the Nuthatch, Wilhelmina the Lesser Spotted Woodpecker, Cora the Cuckoo, Jack the Sparrowhawk, Travis the Tree Creeper, Titus the Tawny Owl, Willow the Willow Tit , and Wilbur the Woodcock.

JACK SPARROWHAWK
RUNA ROBIN
WILFRED GREEN WOODPECKER
CORA CUCKOO
NORA NUTHATCH
WILBUR WOODCOCK
TRAVIS TREECREEPER

Rufus suddenly found himself not just with lots more knowledge, but with more amazing friends in the place that he had for such a long time. He realised that had never really taken enough time to explore beyond his daily life and routines. “Ah the things that we miss out on”, he thought! “We all need to make an effort to go beyond our daily routines and when we only change one little thing every day, it’s not that daunting and difficult anymore”. “What do you know” there is a great method behind this:
Chop it (in yummy size pieces)
Learn it (day by day a little bit)
Experience it (as much as you can)
View (and review everything daily then it sticks better in your memory)
Engage (with others to check and test) and
Repeat it (ideally together with a learning partner)

“C L E V E R – huh?”

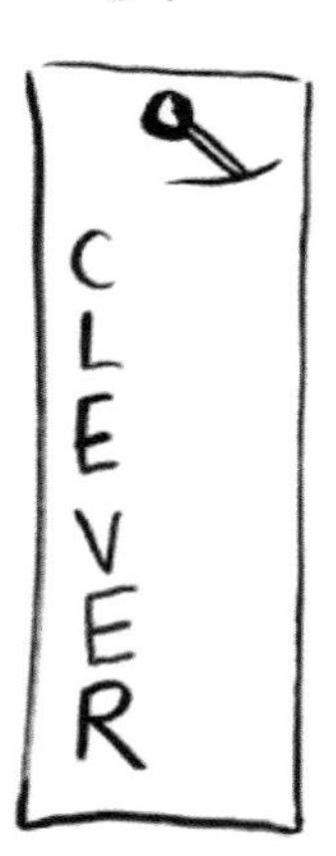

As the friends group grew larger, they researched loads of other things, too. Just then, Rufus remembered that he had realised on the day Archie left, that the stars in the sky change in spring, summer, autumn, and winter. “Why is that?” he asked the group.
Titus the Tiny Tawny Owl raised his wing, “Well,” he said, “If you observe the sky throughout the year, the stars shift ever so gradually to the west. This is because the Earth is circling around our Sun. That is also called the Earth is orbiting around the Sun and it needs one whole year for that”.

“Yes,” remarked Runa the Robin, “And the reason why we get hot summers and cold winters is because of the tilt of the Earth’s axis”. “The what?” , said Randolph.
“The tilt, I mean it’s slightly bent and not straight. Imagine you took an apple and put a twig through the middle of the apple, top to bottom. And then you tilt it…that’s how the Earth circles around the sun.

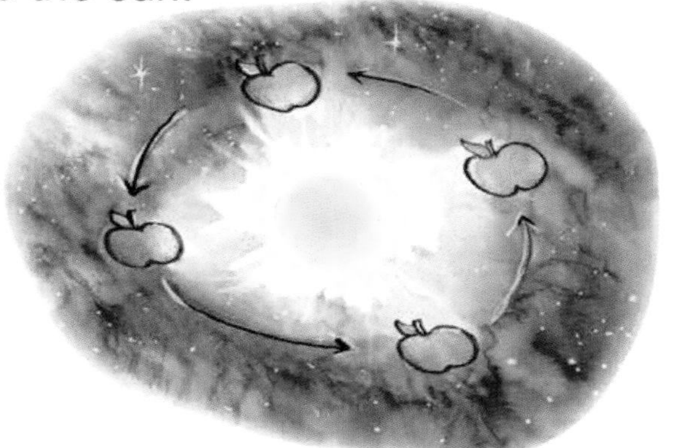

So, when it's nice and warm in our summer, the Earth leans towards the Sun and in our winter, 6 months later, the Earth has travelled half way around the sun and it leans further away. So that way, less of the sun can heat the planet.
So really, the Earth's movement around the sun and the funny tilt cause the four seasons".

"And the earth also circles not in a round circle around the sun, but in a wobbly form, - called an elliptical circle", twittered Cora the Cuckoo with a very bright smile on her face.

"Uh, yes, yes!" said Jack the Sparrowhawk, hopping up and down on his branch. "And the Earth spins on its tilted axis, producing also night and day."

"So," said Rufus, "The four seasons – spring, summer, autumn, and winter happen because the Earth is tilted and the stars change because the Earth moves around the sun within one year"." WOW!", thought Rufus, "I have found new friends, I didn't know learning could be so much fun, and I have found out how you "find" time! I have so much to tell Archie when he comes back, I can't wait!"

With his new friends and his newly changed habits, Rufus life had changed a lot. Together they were all contributing to each other, teaching what they had learned and learning became fun.
Also Rufus started making written plans, just like Archie had told him to. He wrote down his plans in the evening and then focused on carrying them out the next day.

He discovered, that by doing the important things first, he suddenly found more time, just as Archie had said he would. “Crazy! I now have time to read, to meet up with my friends, to study, - and I can still go on my morning run”. “I even still have time to join in the picnics, and do other things that I love, like painting pictures!”

“Amazing,” thought Rufus. “I never thought about my life, or that I could improve it by changing my habits. This whole quiet time has given me a chance to think and change, and I really feel so much stronger and happier. I have made more friends and I have learnt so much! Plus, having learnt to write down my daily priorities means, I don’t forget what needs to be done. And I can even see my progress in the evenings, when I check my daily list. How amazing is that!”

Rufus smiled. “Thank you, Archie,” he said in his thoughts. “I hope you will come and visit again soon, so we can show you just how much you have helped our community, and me.”

Now that Rufus had changed his daily routines, he was no longer having to rush about. With his days better planned, he even found time to enjoy his meals and make them healthier too. Mind you, he was still not very fond of brussels sprouts.
“No,” he thought, “I gave them a try again but I still just don’t like them.”
“But that’s ok,” he said to himself pushing away the fork with a bright grin. “Plenty of other healthy things I love, and I bet I can try out some new ones too”.

Then one day people started coming back to Haste Hill. Not many at first, but life was slowly getting back to 'normal'.

After all Rufus had learned, the squirrel kept up his newly found habits, enjoying his food instead of gobbling it down, eating more of the healthy fresh things the wood had to offer and going for a daily run. He would also meet up with all his old and new friends and still had time to learn and improve his knowledge and study just a little bit every day.

"It's the small steps, that make a huge difference" Rufus thought! "When you start, it can be so overwhelming, but when you break it down into yummy chocolate size bits, then the biggest tasks can be tackled head on!"

He smiled, as he thought of Archie again. How proud Archie would be of him, next time they would meet up!
On top of all of this, Rufus would set and write down his goals, every day and review them in the evening.
"Oh haggard hazelnut", I didn't manage to do the whole list of tasks that I set myself for today, he thought as he was sitting in bed. "But, doesn't matter, tomorrow is another day!" And with that calming thought, he fell asleep with a smile.

Can you imagine that you will remember things better when you write them down?

And you can even make a list not just for one day, but one week, one month or even one year!
Then you break down the big tasks into smaller tasks and work on them every day!
Can you see how you will achieve what you really want to achieve that way?

What do you think you will need? Focus? Yes! Determination, absolutely!
But most of all ..yes ACTION! Just like Rufus. What do you think, can you try this, even start today ?

By the time the people started coming back to the woods, lake, and beach, and life was slowly getting back to “normal”, Rufus really had grown and learned a lot. He had even started running weekend courses for outsiders, to talk about, what living not in ‘haste’ in the countryside was like and how it was good for you.

He would show them the trees and their leaves just like Wilfred had taught him. His courses were so much fun, that soon the word spread, and animals from all over the country came to join Rufus and his friends.

Rufus still lives not far from London, near Haste Hill, but he now takes life just a bit slower. And if you ever go on one of the little trains and drive past Haste Hill, have a look and you just might see a little squirrel. Maybe it's little Rufus showing his friends around the beautiful woods and enjoying every day of his new life.

My Outcomes for .... Day and date ....

1

2

3

4

5

6

7

8

9

10

Printed in Great Britain
by Amazon